Teeth

Written by
Stephen Rickard

Are the teeth of a shark sharp?

Yes, a shark has sharp teeth.

Has a fox got sharp teeth?

Yes, the teeth of a fox are sharp.

Has a cow got sharp teeth?

No, a cow has no sharp teeth.
The teeth are short and fat.

Are the teeth of a duck hard?

A duck has no teeth.
A duck has a bill.

Are the teeth of a rabbit long?

Yes, a rabbit has long teeth.

Has a robin got sharp teeth?

A robin has no teeth.

Are the teeth of a bee hot?

A bee has no teeth.
No bee has hot teeth!

Has a yak got fat teeth?

Fat teeth? No!

Are the teeth of goats red?

No, but if the goat has a pot of jam for dinner, you will see red teeth.

Are the teeth of fish wet?

If a fish has teeth,
they will be wet!

We need good teeth too.

Look at them now.
Are they OK?